HISTORY SPEAKS
PICTURE BOOKS PLUS READER'S THEATER

Enrique Esparza and
THE BATTLE
OF THE ALAMO

BY **SUSAN TAYLOR BROWN**

ILLUSTRATED BY **JENI REEVES**

Ⅿ MILLBROOK PRESS / MINNEAPOLIS

For soldiers everywhere who fight and die for the cause of freedom. And always, for Erik ——STB

For Tegan and Justin, in the words of Graham Nash, "Teach your children well. . . ." ——JR

Millbrook Press
A division of Lerner Publishing Group, Inc.
241 First Avenue North
Minneapolis, MN 55401 U.S.A.

Website address: www.lernerbooks.com

The illustrator thanks models Jalen, Rylan, and Rocio Schunter; John, Lisa, and Otto Peloquin; Kory Kazimour; Greg Newmaster; Stuart and Tegan Reeves; and Justin Croninger. The illustrator also thanks the staff of the Alamo, especially Historian and Curator Dr. Bruce Winders, Librarian Rusty Gamez, and Docent Bill Willeford, as well as the San Antonio Living History Association.

The images in this book are used with the permission of: Texas State Library and Archives Commission, p. 32; © Steve Vidler/SuperStock, p. 33.

Library of Congress Cataloging-in-Publication Data

Brown, Susan Taylor, 1958–
    Enrique Esparza and the battle of the Alamo / by Susan Taylor Brown ; illustrated by Jeni Reeves.
      p. cm. — (History speaks: picture books plus reader's theater)
    Includes bibliographical references.
    ISBN: 978–0–8225–8566–4 (lib. bdg. : alk. paper)
    1. Alamo (San Antonio, Tex.)—Juvenile literature. 2. Alamo (San Antonio, Tex.)—Siege, 1836—Juvenile literature. 3. Texas—History—To 1846—Juvenile literature. 4. San Antonio (Tex.)—Buildings, structures, etc.—Juvenile literature. 5. Esparza, Enrique, 1828–1917—Juvenile literature. I. Reeves, Jeni, ill. II. Title.
F390.B887 2011
976.4'03—dc22

2009049601

Manufactured in the United States of America
2 – CG – 6/1/11

CONTENTS

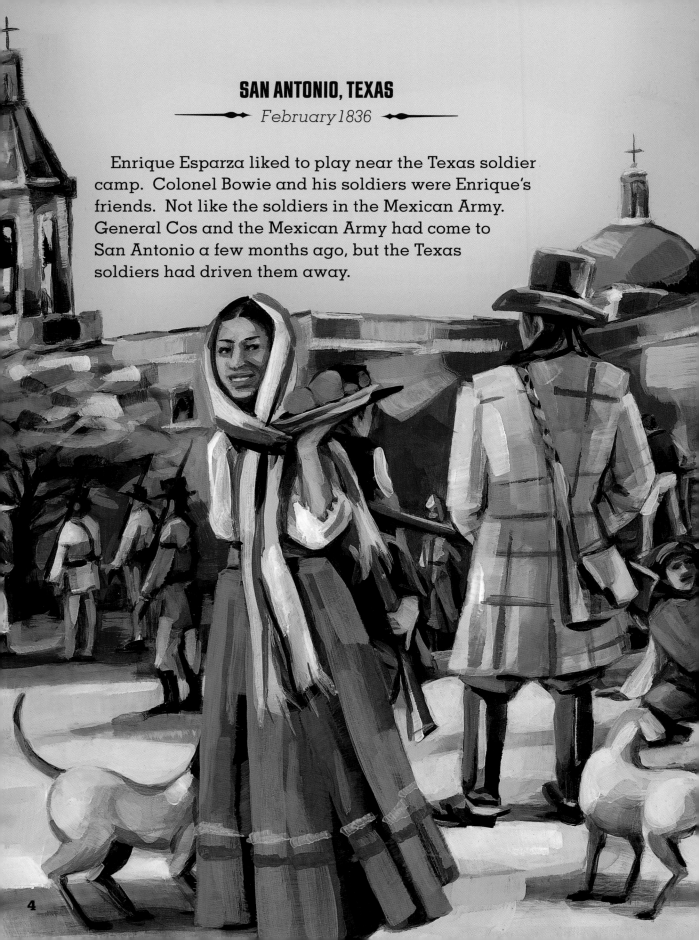

SAN ANTONIO, TEXAS
February 1836

Enrique Esparza liked to play near the Texas soldier camp. Colonel Bowie and his soldiers were Enrique's friends. Not like the soldiers in the Mexican Army. General Cos and the Mexican Army had come to San Antonio a few months ago, but the Texas soldiers had driven them away.

The soldiers taught Enrique American songs with funny words like "Yankee Doodle Dandy." When eight-year-old Enrique sang and danced, the soldiers laughed. Sometimes they gave him a few Mexican coins.

Enrique didn't have time to sing for the soldiers today. His younger brothers played games. But Enrique watched the streets. The Mexican Army was on its way back. Santa Anna was coming with them, and he was angry with the Texans. Enrique's father, Gregorio, told Enrique that the family had to leave San Antonio. John Smith, a good friend, had promised to send a wagon to take them someplace safe.

Gregorio would stay behind. He was a soldier in the Texas Army. Everyone knew the fight against the Mexican Army would take place at a fort called the Alamo. Gregorio was one of the few men who could handle the fort's big cannon.

Enrique and his family were Tejanos. At this time, Texas was part of Mexico. Mexicans who had lived in Texas all their lives were called Tejanos. Most of the people living in Texas were Americans, or Anglos. Some of the Anglos moved to Texas to be free from their government. Many of the Anglos came to Texas for the land. For very little money, they could get many acres of good land to farm with their families.

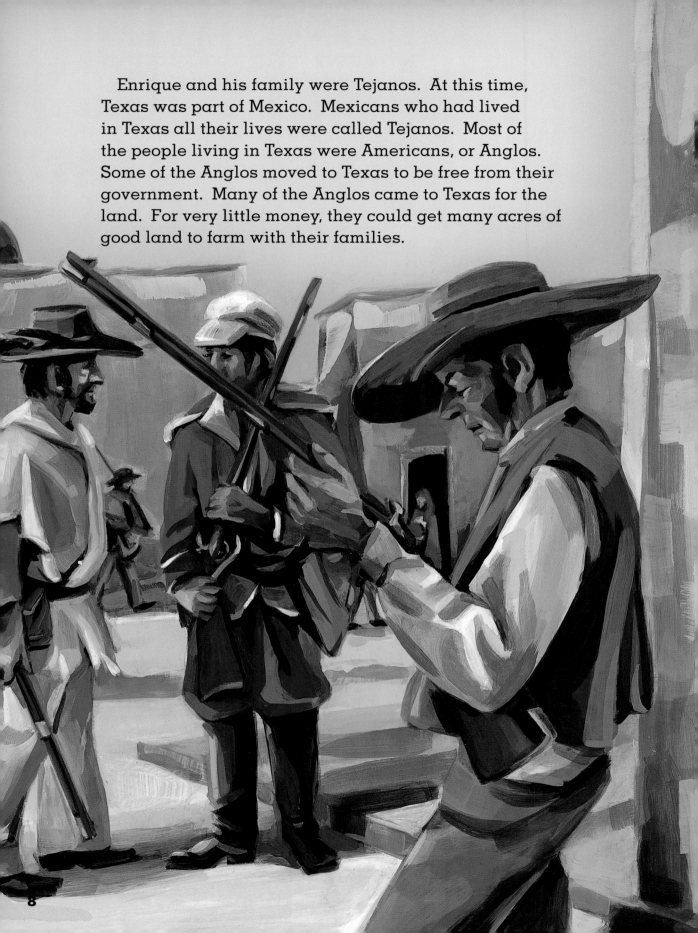

General Antonio López de Santa Anna was the president of Mexico. Many people in Texas did not like him. He raised taxes and passed unfair laws. Santa Anna wanted to teach the Texans a lesson for driving away General Cos.

Enrique waited a long time, but the wagon never arrived. Instead, John Smith came to their house.

"Where is Gregorio?" Mr. Smith asked.

"He is not here," said Anita, Enrique's mother. "Did you bring the wagon?"

"I'm sorry," said Mr. Smith. "It is too late to leave. Tell Gregorio that Santa Anna has arrived."

Enrique ran to tell his sister and brothers. The battle for Texas would soon begin.

"Santa Anna is here!" said Anita when Enrique's father came home.

"Where is the wagon?" asked Gregorio.

"There is no wagon," said Enrique. "Mr. Smith said it was too late."

"I am going to the fort," said Gregorio. "They will need the cannons."

"I will gather our things," said Anita.

"It will be very dangerous," said Enrique's father.

Enrique's mother put her hand on Gregorio's shoulder. "Where you go, I go. If you are to die, I want to be near you."

Enrique wanted to hide, but he knew he should try to be brave too. He stood up straight and tall, just like his father.

Moving to the Alamo took all day. Enrique's family brought a metate to grind corn, a few cooking utensils, and some blankets for sleeping. With every step, Enrique heard the steady beat of Santa Anna's drums. Louder and louder, the drums filled his ears. The soldiers from the Texas Army already stood watch inside the Alamo. Other women and children waited inside too. Enrique's family was the last to arrive.

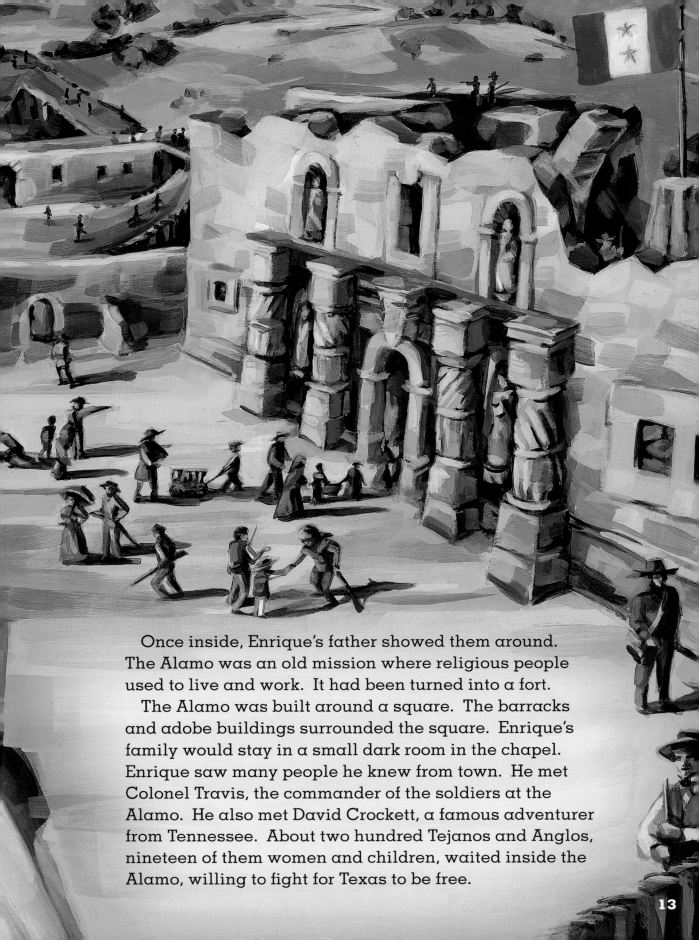

Once inside, Enrique's father showed them around.
The Alamo was an old mission where religious people
used to live and work. It had been turned into a fort.

The Alamo was built around a square. The barracks
and adobe buildings surrounded the square. Enrique's
family would stay in a small dark room in the chapel.
Enrique saw many people he knew from town. He met
Colonel Travis, the commander of the soldiers at the
Alamo. He also met David Crockett, a famous adventurer
from Tennessee. About two hundred Tejanos and Anglos,
nineteen of them women and children, waited inside the
Alamo, willing to fight for Texas to be free.

13

Santa Anna's soldiers hung a blood red flag from the bell tower of San Fernando Cathedral. Even though it was eight hundred yards away, everyone in the Alamo could see it. And everyone knew what it meant. Santa Anna and his soldiers would take no prisoners. They planned to kill anyone who tried to escape or surrender.

"I shall never surrender or retreat!" shouted Colonel Travis. Then he fired a shot from a cannon on the roof of the Alamo. "I will die like a soldier!"

"There will be no surrender," said Gregorio. "We want freedom more than life itself."

Enrique did not want his father to be a soldier. He did not want his father to die.

All night long, Enrique huddled with his family in the corner of the chapel. Darkness filled the fort. Enrique couldn't see anything, but he could hear the guns. He also heard the blasts from the cannon. His body shook, and the darkness and the sound of gunfire filled him.

The fighting continued every day and every night. The
Mexicans fired their cannon into the Alamo every fifteen
minutes. Enrique's heart quaked when the shot tore
through the timbers.

Even though he was afraid, Enrique wanted to help.
If he could find a weapon, he would fight too. Maybe
he could be a hero and save his family. But there were
not enough weapons for everyone. There was even less
ammunition for the rifles and cannons.

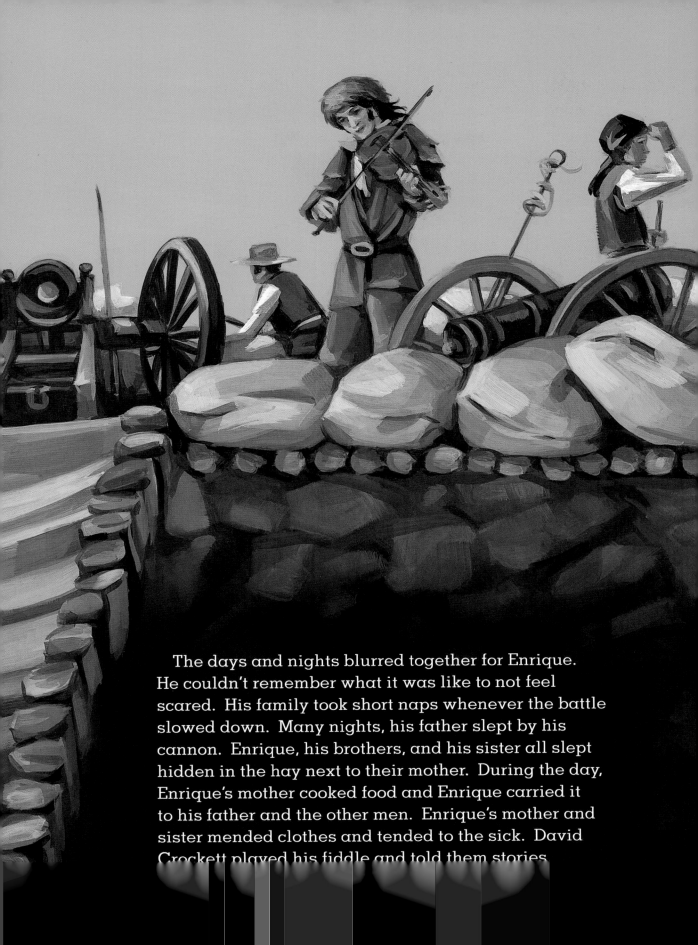

The days and nights blurred together for Enrique. He couldn't remember what it was like to not feel scared. His family took short naps whenever the battle slowed down. Many nights, his father slept by his cannon. Enrique, his brothers, and his sister all slept hidden in the hay next to their mother. During the day, Enrique's mother cooked food and Enrique carried it to his father and the other men. Enrique's mother and sister mended clothes and tended to the sick. David Crockett played his fiddle and told them stories.

Seven days after the fighting began, a message came from Santa Anna. He called for a three-day armistice, a stop to the fighting. People could surrender and leave the Alamo.

David Crockett came to talk to Enrique's father. "You could take your family to safety. Do you want to leave?"

Enrique's lungs burned as he held his breath. What would his father say? People had already died inside the Alamo.

"What will we do?" asked Anita.

"Even if we surrender, I do not think we will be allowed to live. I would rather die fighting." Gregorio shook his head. "Take the children and leave," he said. "I will stay and fight."

"Our family will stay together," said Enrique's mother. "If they kill one, they can kill us all."

"Our freedom is worth fighting for," said Gregorio.

Enrique did not think he could possibly feel more scared. But he did.

Day after day, the Anglos and the Tejanos fought hard. They were almost out of ammunition. They were hungry and thirsty. Some men were so tired they fell asleep on guard.

After twelve long days and nights, the attacks stopped. It grew quiet. Enrique wondered if Santa Anna's army had given up fighting or was planning an even bigger attack. He curled up next to his mother and father and fell asleep.

Suddenly, a terrible noise exploded into the darkness.

"Gregorio," said Anita, "the soldiers have jumped the wall."

Enrique's father raced off to join the battle.

Santa Anna's soldiers tore through the fort. They fired everywhere. They threw open the door to the chapel. Smoke filled the air, but Enrique stayed hidden in the hay.

As the fighting went on, another group of Mexican soldiers rushed into the chapel. Enrique felt sick. He wondered if he was about to die. He shut his eyes, opened them, and then shut them again. The soldiers fired. Bullets whizzed past and missed them all. Enrique ran to the corner of the chapel with the rest of the children and their mothers. He hoped the shooting would stop soon.

At daylight, soldiers came to search the chapel's rooms. One soldier poked Enrique's mother with his bayonet.

"Where is your money?" he yelled.

"I have no money," said Enrique's mother.

The soldier slapped her, and she screamed. Enrique wanted to scream too.

"Leave them alone!" yelled another soldier. "The women and children are not to be hurt."

"Take them to the house in the plaza," said a third soldier.

Enrique's mother herded the family through the Alamo. She guided them toward the plaza. The smoke was thick and burned Enrique's eyes. He saw dead bodies of Anglos and Tejanos, but he tried not to look at them.

For most of the day, Enrique waited with the rest of the women and children. Then the soldiers told them Santa Anna wanted to see them. Enrique was worried. What would Santa Anna do to the rest of his family now? Enrique's mother waited her turn. She held Enrique's sister's hand. One of Enrique's brothers held onto her dress. Enrique tried his best to stand up straight and tall like his father.

"What is your name?" asked Santa Anna.
Enrique's mother looked very brave as she spoke.
"Anita Esparza."
"Where is your husband?"
"He's dead at the Alamo."

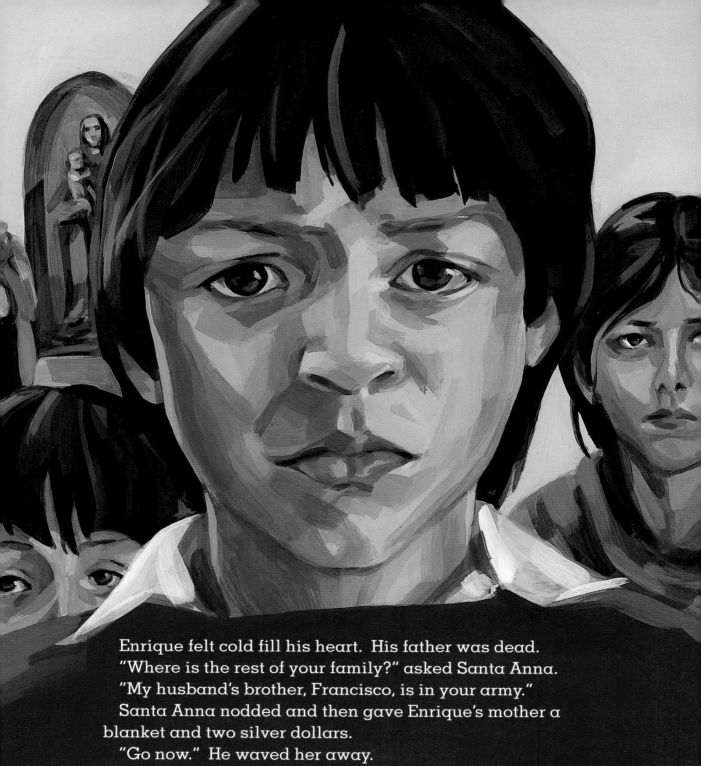

Enrique felt cold fill his heart. His father was dead.
"Where is the rest of your family?" asked Santa Anna.
"My husband's brother, Francisco, is in your army."
Santa Anna nodded and then gave Enrique's mother a
blanket and two silver dollars.
"Go now." He waved her away.
There was nothing Enrique could do. He clenched his hands
tightly at his side and stared at the man who killed his father.
He would never forget the face of Santa Anna. It would haunt
him the rest of his life, even years later when Texas and all the

ENRIQUE ESPARZA

Author's Note

Life in Texas in the 1830s was hard. Texas was part of Mexico, but Texas and Mexico often fought. More than twenty thousand people had come to Texas from the United States. They wanted to be independent. About four thousand Tejanos also lived in Texas. They had to choose whether to fight for Texas or Mexico. Gregorio Esparza fought with the Anglos at the Alamo. But his brother Francisco fought with the Mexicans.

The battle of the Alamo started on February 23, 1836. It ended on March 6. Santa Anna's army had about 1,800 soldiers. There were fewer than two hundred fighters inside Alamo. About 189 Texans and 1,600 Mexican soldiers were killed in the fighting.

A few of the men who died at the Alamo are famous. Colonel Jim Bowie was a skilled knife fighter and treasure seeker. David Crockett, known in modern times as Davy, was a former congressman from Tennessee. His adventures on the frontier made him well known to many Americans.

The battle at the Alamo was not the end of the fighting between Texas and Mexico. On April 21, 1836, Sam Houston

THE ALAMO

led the Texans into the battle of San Jacinto. Houston said, "Remember the Alamo." This time, the Texans won. The day after the battle, Santa Anna was captured. As a prisoner, he signed peace treaties. The Republic of Texas became an independent country for a time. On December 29, 1845, Congress admitted Texas to the United States.

After the battle of the Alamo, Enrique and his brothers worked on nearby farms. For many years, Enrique farmed about 33 miles (53 kilometers) south of San Antonio. As he grew older, he lived with his son in Losoya, Texas. Enrique Esparza died on December 20, 1917. He is buried in Losoya.

Performing Reader's Theater

Dear Student,

Reader's Theater is a dramatic reading. It is a little like a play, but you don't need to memorize your lines. Here are some tips that will help you do your best in a Reader's Theater performance.

BEFORE THE PERFORMANCE

- **Choose your part:** Your teacher may assign parts, or you may be allowed to choose your own part. The character you play does not need to be the same age as you. A boy can play the part of a girl, and a girl can play the part of a boy. That's why it's called acting!

- **Find your lines:** Your character's name is always the same color. The name at the bottom of each page tells you which character has the first line on the next page. If you are allowed to write on your script, highlight your lines. If you cannot write on the script, you may want to use sticky flags to mark your lines.

- **Check pronunciations of words:** If your character's lines include any words you aren't sure how to pronounce, check the pronunciation guide on page 45. If a word isn't there or you still aren't sure how to say it, check a dictionary or ask a teacher, librarian, or other adult.

- **Use your emotions:** Think about how your character feels in the story. If you imagine how your character feels, the audience will hear the emotion in your voice.

- **Use your imagination:** Think about how your character's voice might sound. For example, an old man's voice will sound different from a baby's voice. If you do change your voice, make sure the audience can still understand the words you are saying.

- **Practice your lines:** Even though you do not need to memorize your lines, you should still be comfortable reading them. Read your lines aloud often so they flow smoothly.

DURING THE PERFORMANCE

- **Keep your script away from your face but high enough to read:** If you cover your face with your script, you block your voice from the audience. If you have your script too low, you need to tip your head down farther to read it and the audience won't be able to hear you.

- **Use eye contact:** Good Reader's Theater performers look at the audience as much as they look at their scripts. If you look down, the sound of your voice goes down to the script and not out to the audience.

- **Speak clearly:** Make sure you are loud enough. Say all your words carefully. Be sure not to read too quickly. Remember, if you feel nervous, you may start to speak faster than usual.

- **Use facial expressions and gestures:** Your facial expressions and gestures (hand movements) help the audience know how your character is feeling. If your character is happy, smile. If your character is angry, cross your arms and be sure not to smile.

- **Have fun:** It's okay if you feel nervous. If you make a mistake, just try to relax and keep going. Reader's Theater is meant to be fun for the actors and the audience!

Cast of Characters

NARRATOR 1

NARRATOR 2

ENRIQUE ESPARZA:
an eight-year-old boy

ANITA ESPARZA:
Enrique's mother

GREGORIO ESPARZA:
Enrique's father

READER 1:
Mr. Smith, Mexican soldier

READER 2:
Colonel Travis,
another Mexican soldier, Santa Anna

ALL:
Everyone except sound

SOUND:
This part has no lines. The person in this role
is in charge of the sound effects.
Find the sound effects for this script
at www.lerneresource.com.

The Script

NARRATOR 1: Welcome to San Antonio, Texas. It is February 1836, and Texas is part of Mexico. The story you are about to hear is the true story of the Esparza family.

ENRIQUE: I am Enrique Esparza, and I am eight years old. I live with my parents, my sister, and my brothers. We are all Tejanos.

NARRATOR 1: Tejanos were Mexicans who had lived in Texas all their lives. Most of the people living in Texas were Americans, also called Anglos. Some of them had come to be free from their government. Many had come to get good land they could farm with their families.

GREGORIO: I am Enrique's father, Gregorio. I am a soldier in the Texas Army.

ENRIQUE: He is one of the only men who can handle the big cannon at the Alamo.

ANITA: *Hola*, I am Enrique's mother, Anita.

ENRIQUE: I have heard my mother and father talking a lot about someone named Santa Anna.

NARRATOR 2: General Antonio López de Santa Anna was the president of Mexico. Many people in Texas did not like him. He raised taxes and passed unfair laws. The Mexican Army had come to San Antonio a few months ago, but the Texas soldiers had driven it away. Now the Mexican Army was on its way back. Santa Anna was coming too, and he was angry with the Texans.

Next Page — **ALL**

ALL: Everyone knew the fight against Santa Anna would happen at the Alamo.

GREGORIO: Anita, you must take the children and leave San Antonio. It will be very dangerous here. Our friend John Smith has promised to send a wagon to take you someplace safe. I will stay behind at the Alamo to fight.

NARRATOR 1: Sadly, the family's plans had to change.

SOUND: [knock on door]

ENRIQUE: Mother, Mr. Smith is here!

ANITA: Thank you, Enrique. Hello, Mr. Smith.

READER 1 (as Mr. Smith): Where is your husband?

ANITA: He is not here. Did you bring the wagon?

READER 1 (as Mr. Smith): I'm sorry. It is too late to leave. Tell Gregorio that Santa Anna has already arrived.

NARRATOR 1: Enrique ran to tell his sister and brothers the news.

NARRATOR 2: The battle for Texas would soon begin.

NARRATOR 1: Later that day, Gregorio returned home.

ANITA: Oh, Gregorio, Santa Anna is already here!

GREGORIO: Where is the wagon?

ENRIQUE: There is no wagon. Mr. Smith said it was too late.

Next Page — **GREGORIO**

GREGORIO: Then I am going to the fort. They will need the cannons.

ANITA: I will gather our things.

GREGORIO: It will be very dangerous.

ANITA: Where you go, I go. If you are to die, I want to be near you.

ENRIQUE: I wish I could hide, but I know I must be brave.

NARRATOR 1: Moving to the Alamo took all day. Enrique's family brought a metate to grind corn, a few cooking utensils, and some blankets for sleeping. They could hear the steady pounding of Santa Anna's drums in the distance.

SOUND: [drums pounding]

NARRATOR 2: Soldiers from the Texas Army already stood watch at the Alamo. Other women and children waited inside too. Enrique's family was the last to arrive.

NARRATOR 1: The Alamo was filled with about two hundred people. Enrique saw many people he knew from town. He met Colonel Travis.

READER 2 (as Colonel Travis): Hello, Enrique. I am Colonel Travis. I am in charge of the soldiers here. You and your family will stay in the chapel, where you will be safe.

ANITA: Look! Do you see that flag?

Next Page — **NARRATOR 1**

NARRATOR 1: Santa Anna's soldiers hung a blood red flag from the bell tower of San Fernando Cathedral. Everyone in the Alamo could see it in the distance.

NARRATOR 2: The flag meant Santa Anna and his soldiers would take no prisoners. They planned to kill anyone who tried to escape or surrender.

READER 2 (as Colonel Travis): I shall never surrender or retreat! I will die like a soldier!

NARRATOR 1: Colonel Travis fired a shot from a cannon on the roof of the Alamo.

SOUND: [cannon firing]

GREGORIO: There will be no surrender. We want freedom more than life itself.

ENRIQUE: I wish my father was not a soldier. I don't want him to die.

NARRATOR 1: That night, Enrique huddled with his family in the corner of the chapel. Darkness filled the fort. Enrique couldn't see anything, but he could hear the guns and the cannons.

SOUND: [guns and cannons]

NARRATOR 2: The fighting continued every day and every night. The Mexican Army fired its cannon into the Alamo every fifteen minutes. Many nights, Enrique's father slept by his cannon. The rest of the family slept hidden in the hay next to their mother in the chapel.

Next Page — **ENRIQUE**

ENRIQUE: I want to help the soldiers. If I can find a weapon, I will fight too. Maybe I can be a hero and save my family.

NARRATOR 1: But there were not enough weapons for everyone. There was even less ammunition for the rifles and cannons.

NARRATOR 2: During the day, the soldiers and their families had many things to do. People took short naps and tried to relax whenever the battle slowed down. Sometimes David Crocket, a famous adventurer from Tennessee, played his fiddle.

SOUND: [fiddle playing]

ANITA: Enrique, go and take this food to your father and the others. Hurry back so you can help me with the wounded men.

NARRATOR 1: Seven days after the fighting began, a message came from Santa Anna. He called for a three-day armistice. During this stop in the fighting, people could surrender and leave the Alamo.

ANITA: What will we do? Is it really safe to leave?

GREGORIO: Even if we surrender, I do not think we will be allowed to live. I would rather die fighting. Please take the children and leave. I will stay and fight.

ANITA: Our family will stay together. If they kill one, they can kill us all.

GREGORIO: Our freedom is worth fighting for.

Next Page — **NARRATOR 2**

NARRATOR 2: The armistice ended. Day after day, the Anglos and the Tejanos in the Alamo fought hard against the Mexican Army. Supplies were running low. The Texas soldiers were almost out of ammunition. Everyone was hungry and thirsty. Some men were so tired they fell asleep while guarding the fort.

NARRATOR 1: After twelve long days and nights, the attacks stopped.

ENRIQUE: Mother, it's so quiet. Maybe the fighting is done.

NARRATOR 1: Suddenly, a terrible noise exploded into the darkness.

SOUND: [guns and cannons]

ANITA: Gregorio, wake up. Santa Anna's soldiers have jumped the wall!

NARRATOR 2: Santa Anna's soldiers tore through the fort. They fired everywhere. They threw open the door to the chapel. Enrique felt sick. He wondered if he was about to die. He shut his eyes. The soldiers fired their weapons.

NARRATOR 1: Bullets whizzed past the women and children, but the bullets missed them all. Enrique ran to the corner of the chapel and huddled with the rest of his family.

NARRATOR 2: At daylight, soldiers searched the chapel's rooms. One soldier poked Enrique's mother with his bayonet.

READER 1 (as a Mexican soldier): Where is your money?

Next Page — **ANITA**

ANITA: I have no money.

NARRATOR 1: The soldier slapped her.

SOUND: [slap]

ANITA: [scream]

NARRATOR 2: Enrique wanted to scream too.

READER 2 (as another Mexican soldier): Leave them alone! The women and children are not to be hurt. Take them to the house in the plaza.

NARRATOR 2: Enrique and his family walked through the Alamo toward the plaza. The smoke was thick and burned Enrique's eyes. He saw dead bodies of Anglos and Tejanos, but he tried not to look at them.

READER 1 (AS A MEXICAN SOLDIER): Santa Anna wants to see you.

ENRIQUE: What will General Santa Anna do to us?

READER 2 (as Santa Anna): I am General Santa Anna. What is your name?

ANITA: Anita Esparza.

READER 2 (as Santa Anna): Where is your husband?

ANITA: He's dead at the Alamo.

READER 2 (as Santa Anna): Where is the rest of your family?

Next Page — **ANITA**

ANITA: My husband's brother, Francisco, is in your army.

NARRATOR 1: Santa Anna nodded and gave Enrique's mother a blanket and two silver dollars.

READER 2 (as Santa Anna): You can go now.

NARRATOR 2: There was nothing Enrique could do. He clenched his hands tightly at his side and stared at the man who killed his father. It would haunt him the rest of his life, even years later when Texas and all the Tejanos were free from Mexico.

ALL: The End

Pronunciation Guide

adobe: uh-DOH-bee

Anglos: ANG-glohz

Antonio López de Santa Anna: ahn-TOH-nee-oh LOH-pehz day SAHN-tah AH-nah

armistice: ARM-iss-tiss

barracks: BARE-uhks

bayonet: BAY-uh-net

Bowie: BOH-ee

colonel: KUR-nuhl

Cos: KOHS

Enrique: ehn-REE-kay

Esparza: es-PAHR-zuh

Gregorio: gray-GORE-ee-oh

metate: muh-TAH-tee

quaked: kwaykt

Tejanos: tay-HAH-nos

Glossary

adobe: bricks made from clay mixed with straw and dried in the sun

ammunition: things that can be fired from weapons, such as bullets and cannonballs

Anglos: Americans living in Texas during the 1830s

armistice: a stop in fighting during a war

barracks: one or more buildings where soldiers live

bayonet: a long knife attached to the end of a rifle

colonel: an officer in the army ranking below a general

fiddle: a violin

metate: a stone tool used for grinding corn

mission: a church or other place where priests and nuns live and work

plaza: an open area surrounded by buildings

quaked: shook with fear

surrender: to give up a fight

Tejanos: Mexicans living in Texas during the 1830s

Selected Bibliography

Hansen, Todd, ed. *The Alamo Reader: A Study in History.* Mechanicsburg, PA: Stackpole Books, 2003.

Lord, Walter. *A Time to Stand: The Epic of the Alamo.* Lincoln: University of Nebraska Press, 1978.

Matovina, Timothy M. *The Alamo Remembered: Tejano Accounts and Perspectives.* Austin: University of Texas Press, 1995.

Ragsdale, Crystal Sasse. *The Women and Children of the Alamo.* Austin, TX: State House Press, 1994.

Roberts, Randy, and James S. Olson. *A Line in the Sand: The Alamo in Blood and Memory.* New York: Free Press, 2001.

Further Reading and Websites

BOOKS

Adams, Simon, and David Murdoch. *Texas.* New York: DK Publishing, 2003.

Text, photographs, and artwork present the history of Texas.

Collard, Sneed B., III. *David Crockett: Fearless Frontiersman.* New York: Marshall Cavendish Benchmark, 2007.

This biography introduces the life story of David Crockett.

Fradin, Dennis Brindell. *The Alamo.* New York: Marshall Cavendish, 2007.

This book provides a straightforward overview of events leading up to the battle at the Alamo.

Jakes, John. *Susanna of the Alamo: A True Story*. San Diego: Guilliver Books, 1986.
Discover the story of Susanna Dickenson, an Anglo woman who survived with her baby inside the Alamo.

Nelson, Kristin L. *The Alamo*. Minneapolis: Lerner Publications Company, 2010.
Text and photographs give readers an up-close look at the history, significance, and story behind the famous fort.

Tanaka, Shelley. *The Alamo: Surrounded and Outnumbered, They Chose to Make a Defiant Last Stand*. New York: Hyperion Books for Children, 2003.
Read about the events of the Alamo as well as Santa Anna, James Bowie, and other key fighters from both sides of the battle.

WEBSITES

Just for Kids
http://www.thealamo.org/just_for_kids.html
The Alamo's website includes a section for kids featuring an Alamo memory game, a word find, and a crossword puzzle. Other sections of the site include information about the battle and visiting the Alamo.

Kids Only
http://www.texasbeyondhistory.net/kids/index.html
This site from the University of Texas at Austin provides games, trivia, activities, and more, all focused on Texas history.

San Jacinto Museum of History
http://www.sanjacinto-museum.org/
This site offers information about the Battle of San Jacinto, which took place in April 1836. Sam Houston and his army defeated Santa Anna in this battle.

Dear Teachers and Librarians,

Congratulations on bringing Reader's Theater to your students! Reader's Theater is an excellent way for your students to develop their reading fluency. Phrasing and inflection, two important reading skills, are at the heart of Reader's Theater. Students also develop public speaking skills such as volume, pacing, and facial expression.

The traditional format of Reader's Theater is very simple. There really is no right or wrong way to do it. By following these few tips, you and your students will be ready to explore the world of Reader's Theater.

EQUIPMENT

Location: A theater or gymnasium is a fine place for a Reader's Theater performance, but staging the performance in the classroom works well too.

Scripts: Each reader will need a copy of the script. Scripts that are individually printed should be bound into binders that allow the readers to turn the pages easily. Printable scripts for all the books in this series are available at www.historyspeaksbooks.com.

Music Stands: Music stands are very helpful for the readers to set their scripts on.

Costumes: Traditional Reader's Theater does not use costumes. Dressing uniformly, such as all wearing the same color shirt, will give a group a polished look. Specific costume pieces can be used when a reader is performing multiple roles. They help the audience follow the story.

Props: Props are optional. If necessary, readers may mime or gesture to convey objects that are important to the story. Props can be used much like a costume piece to identify different characters performed by one reader. Prop suggestions for each story are available at www.historyspeaksbooks.com.

Background and Sound Effects: These aren't essential, but they can add to the fun of Reader's Theater. Customized backgrounds for each story in this series and sound effects corresponding to the scripts are available at www.historyspeaksbooks.com. You will need a screen or electronic whiteboard for the background. You will need a computer with speakers to play the sound effects.

PERFORMANCE

Staging: Readers usually face the audience in a straight line or a semicircle. If the readers are using music stands, the stands should be raised chest high. A stand should not block a reader's mouth or face, but it should allow for the reader to read without looking down too much. The main character is usually placed in the center. The narrator is on the end. In the case of multiple narrators, place one narrator on each end.

Reading: Reader's Theater scripts do not need to be memorized. However, the readers should be familiar enough with the script to maintain a fair amount of eye contact with the audience. Encourage readers to act with their voices by reading with inflection and emotion.

Blocking (stage movement): For traditional Reader's Theater, there are no blocking cues to follow. You may want to have the students turn the pages simultaneously. Some groups prefer that readers sit or turn their back to the audience when their characters are "offstage" or have left a scene. Some groups will have their readers move about the stage, script in hand, to interact with the other readers. The choice is up to you.

Overture and Curtain Call: Before the performance, a member of the group should announce the title and the author of the piece. At the end of the performance, all readers step in front of their music stands, stand in a line, grasp hands, and bow in unison.

LERNER
SOURCE

Please visit www.lernerresource.com for printable scripts, prop suggestions, sound effects, a background image that can be projected on a screen or electronic whiteboard, a Reader's Theater teacher's guide, and reading-level information for all roles.